GRANDPA
AT THE
BEACH

Rob Le

MONDO

First published in the United States of America in 1998
by **MONDO Publishing**

Originally published in the United Kingdom in 1997
by The Bodley Head Children's Books,
an imprint of Random House UK Ltd.

For information contact:
MONDO Publishing
980 Avenue of the Americas

New York, NY 10018

Visit our website at http://www.mondopub.com

Printed in China
First Mondo Printing, August 1997

07   9 8 7 6 5 4 3

Library of Congress Cataloging-in-Publication Data

Lewis, Rob, 1962–
    Grandpa at the beach/ Rob Lewis.
        p.   cm.
    "Originally published in the United Kingdom in 1997 by the Bodley
Head Children's Books, an imprint of Random House UK Ltd."—Copyr. p.
    Summary: Finley and Grandpa have various adventures when the family
takes a vacation at the beach.
    ISBN 1-57255-552-1 (pbk : alk. paper)
    [1. Beaches—Fiction.   2. Grandfathers—Fiction.   3. Vacations—Fiction.
4. Bears—Fiction]   I. Title.
PZ7.L58785Gp   1998
[E]—dc21   97-11753
                                                              CIP
                                                               AC

THE
BEACH HOUSE

Grandpa, Finley, Dad, and
Mom were going on a vacation.
They were driving to a house
by the sea.
It was raining hard.
Everyone was gloomy.
"I hope it doesn't rain the whole
time," said Finley.
"I will tell a story to cheer us up,"
said Grandpa.

Grandpa told a scary story.

"A monster with bat wings banged at the door," said Grandpa, "but the door was locked . . ."

Finley looked out the window.

The sky was getting darker and darker.

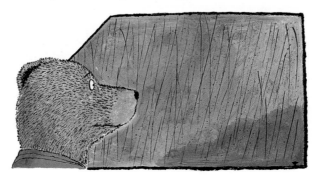

"So the monster went to the back door and turned the door handle," said Grandpa, "and the door opened ..."

Dad switched on the headlights.

"And the monster stomped up the stairs," continued Grandpa, "and opened the closet door..."

"This must be the beach house," said Mom.

Dad stopped the car.

"I will get the key from the house next door," he said.

"I will come, too," said Mom. "The beach house looks scary in the dark." "We're not scared!" said Grandpa and Finley. "We will stay here." Grandpa and Finley sat in the car.

"Let's see if the beach house is open,"
said Grandpa.

"We should wait for Mom and Dad,"
said Finley.

"You're not *scared*, are you?" asked
Grandpa.

"No," said Finley.

They tried to open the front door.

It was locked.

"I will check the back door," said
Finley.

The back door was open.

"I will play a trick on Grandpa," said
Finley. "Then we will see if Grandpa
is scared."

Grandpa waited on the porch.

He heard a noise.

it went.

Grandpa was scared.

"I will look for Finley," he said.

Grandpa went to the back door.

"Boo!"

shouted Finley.

"I wasn't scared," said Grandpa.

"This is an old house," said Finley.

"There are no lights."

"I will find some candles," said Grandpa.

But Grandpa did not find any candles.

Instead he found a bag of flour.

"I will play a trick on Finley," he said.

Finley was in the living room.

He heard a noise upstairs.

"Grrrrrrr!"

it went.

Finley was scared.

Finley went upstairs to look.

"Boo!"

shouted Grandpa, jumping out of a closet.

"I wasn't scared," said Finley.

Suddenly there was a loud bang on
the front door.

Someone was trying to get in.

"It's only Mom and Dad," said Finley.

"But Mom and Dad have the keys!"
said Grandpa.

It was the monster with bat wings.

Grandpa *and* Finley were scared.

The monster went to the back door
and turned the handle.

The door opened.

Grandpa and Finley hid in the closet.

The monster stomped up the stairs,

and opened the closet door . . .

"Sorry to scare you," said Dad.

"This is the wrong house. Our beach house is further down the road."

"We weren't scared!" said Grandpa and Finley, trembling.

STICKY PICNIC

It was a hot day.

"Let's have a picnic," said Finley.

"Okay," said Mom.

Mom made a cake.

Finley washed
some lettuce.

Grandpa made lots of
honey sandwiches.
They were very sticky.

Dad drove everyone to the beach.

Mom spread out a tablecloth.

Grandpa put out the sandwiches.
The honey sandwiches had made
everything sticky.

They started to eat. Flies buzzed
around the honey sandwiches.

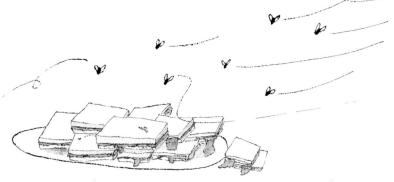

"Go away, flies," said Finley.

Grandpa tried to hit them with his paper.

He missed the flies and hit Mom's

cake.

Then gulls came to steal the honey
sandwiches.

"Keep off, gulls," said Dad.

Mom waved them away with a towel.
She missed the gulls but hit Finley's
lemonade.

Then wasps flew around the sandwiches.

"Get lost, wasps!" shouted Grandpa.

Finley swatted the wasps with his hat.

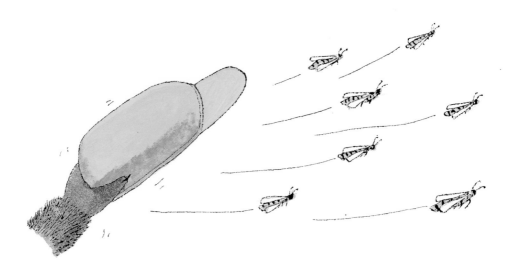

He hit one wasp but another one
stung Dad.

"Aaah!"

yelled Dad. "These sandwiches are
trouble."

"I will move them," said Grandpa.

Grandpa moved the sandwiches.

Finley mopped up his lemonade.

Mom cut the cake.

And Dad nursed his wasp sting.

It started to rain.

"Oh no!" they cried. They picked
up all the food and got into the car.
They ate and watched the rain.

"At least we are dry," said Grandpa.

"And there are no flies or gulls,"
said Finley.

"Or wasps," said Dad.

Mom looked down.

Something was crawling up her leg.

"Ants!" she said.

Mom looked at Grandpa.

"Where did you put those honey
sandwiches?" she asked.

"Um . . ." said Grandpa, worried.

"I think you're sitting on them!"

THE
AIR MATTRESS

Grandpa and Finley found a cove.

"You go explore," said Grandpa.

"I will stay here and sunbathe."

"I want to sunbathe, too," said Finley.

"I will lie on the air mattress,"
said Grandpa.

"You can lie on the pebbles."

"But Mom said I could lie on the air
mattress," said Finley.

"I am old and creaky," said Grandpa.

"I need a soft place to lie down."

Grandpa pretended to be old
and creaky.

Finley didn't want to sunbathe on the pebbles. He decided to explore the cove instead.

Finley looked under a stone and found a crab.

He looked in a rock pool and found a starfish and some long, green, slimy seaweed.

He put them in a pail.

"Look, Grandpa," said Finley.

Grandpa's eyes were closed.

"Very nice," said Grandpa.

"I will look for more things," said Finley.

"Don't go too far," said Grandpa.

"The sea can be dangerous."

Grandpa was very comfortable on the air mattress. It was like floating on a cloud. Soon he was fast asleep.

But when Grandpa opened his eyes he found he was floating on water. The air mattress had drifted out to sea.

Grandpa paddled towards the shore.
But a strong wind blew him further
out.

Soon Grandpa could not see the land.

"HELP!"

he shouted.

The wind became stronger.

The waves grew bigger.

The clouds got darker.

Soon Grandpa was in the middle of a big storm. Thunder was rumbling across the sky. Waves were crashing over him. The air mattress began to sink.

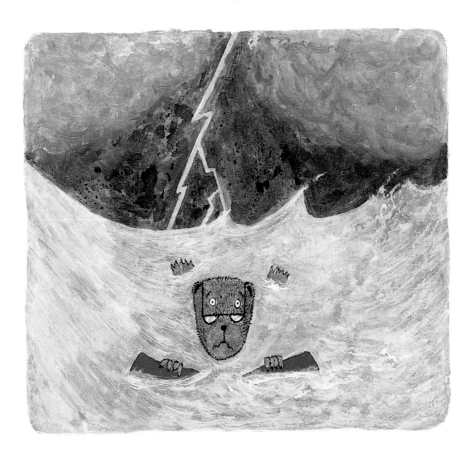

Suddenly out of the waves came long, green, slimy tentacles.

Then came two big eyes and two big claws.

"Help!" cried Grandpa. "It's a sea monster."

"Sorry, Grandpa," said Finley.

"My pail fell over."

Grandpa woke up.

Finley took away the seaweed.

The crab started to scuttle away.

"I will put the crab and the starfish
back in the sea," said Finley.
"You can go back to sleep now."

"I have changed my mind," said Grandpa. "You can have the air mattress and *I* will go explore!"